Second Grade Rocks!

by Judy Katschke
illustrated by Clare Elsom

Scholastic Inc.

ISBN 978-0-545-82338-8

Text copyright © 2015 by Judy Katschke
Illustrations copyright © 2015 by Clare Elsom

Published by Scholastic Inc. SCHOLASTIC and associated logos are trademarks and/or registered trademarks of Scholastic Inc.

10 9 8 7 6 5 4 3 2   15 16 17 18 19/0

Printed in the U.S.A.   40

First printing, May 2015

It was the last day of school.
"Hey, guess what?" Kono said.
"Today is the last day of first grade!"
"The last day of first grade?" Andrew
said. "Forever?"

The classroom looked like a carnival.
Ms. Fickle sat inside a little booth.
Today she was dressed as a
fortune-teller.

"I can see the future," Ms. Fickle said.
"I see you all in second grade!"
"Cool!" Colin, Molly, Kono, Julia, and
Josh cheered.
"Not cool," Andrew said.

"Now it's your turn to see the future," Ms. Fickle said. "What will you be like in second grade?"

Ms. Fickle passed out paper and
crayons.
"Ready? Set? Draw!" she said.
Everyone began to draw.
Everyone but Andrew.

Andrew wasn't ready or set.
He didn't want to draw himself in
second grade.
He didn't even want to *think* about
second grade.

But Julia did! She couldn't wait for second grade.
"Second grade will be great," Julia said. "And so will I!"

"When I'm in second grade, I'll read more books than ever!" Julia said.

"I'll build a huge tower of books all the way to the sky!"

WELCOME TO JULIA'S WORLD-FAMOUS LEANING TOWER OF BOOKS!

Andrew fed Nibbles, the class pet.
He still didn't want to think about
second grade.

But Colin did! He couldn't wait for second grade.
"Second grade will be awesome," Colin said. "And so will I!"

"When I'm in second grade, I'll be tall enough to do a slam dunk!" Colin said.

"And at lunchtime, I'll be able to reach the best desserts. Yum!"

Andrew watered the class plants.
He still didn't want to think about
second grade.

But Kono did! She couldn't wait for second grade.

"Second grade will be totally cool," Kono said. "And so will I!"

"When I'm in second grade, I'll star in the class play!" Kono said.

"I'll make the costumes, paint the sets, play the music, and even pull the curtain when it's showtime!"

CURTAIN BY KONO!

STARRING... KONO!

Andrew rested his head on his desk.
He still didn't want to think about
second grade.

But Josh did! He couldn't wait for
second grade.
"Second grade will be SWEET!"
Josh said. "And so will I!"

"When I'm in second grade, I'll be bigger, and so will my ant farm," Josh said.

"Ant City will have skyscrapers, bridges, and even its own baseball team. GO CRAWLERS!"

Andrew sharpened a pile of pencils.
He still didn't want to think about
second grade.

But Molly did! She couldn't wait for second grade.
"Second grade will be out of this world!" Molly said. "And so will I!"

"When I'm in second grade, I'll build a robot for the science fair," Molly said.

"My robot will talk, walk, and play kickball. It will even clean the pet cage!"

Andrew did everything NOT to think about second grade.
He popped buckets of popcorn.
He even spun the prize wheel until he got dizzy!

"Where's *your* picture, Andrew?"
Colin asked.
"Don't you want to go to second
grade?" Kono asked.
"No," said Andrew. "Never!"
"Why not?" Josh asked.

"Because!" Andrew shouted. "Then we won't be first-grade friends anymore!"

"That's true, Andrew," Ms. Fickle said. "You won't be first-grade friends . . ."

". . . You'll be <u>second-grade</u> friends!"
Andrew smiled.

Then he raced to his desk and drew
himself in second grade.

He put Colin, Molly, Kono, Julia, and
Josh in his picture, too.

"Second grade is going to rock," Andrew said. "And so are we!" **"SECOND GRADE, HERE WE COME!!"** the kids cheered.

ANDREW